Something Queer at the Haunted School

YEARLING BOOKS/YOUNG YEARLINGS/YEARLING CLASSICS are designed especially to entertain and enlighten young people. Patricia Reilly Giff, consultant to this series, received the bachelor's degree from Marymount College. She holds the master's degree in history from St. John's University, and a Professional Diploma in Reading from Hofstra University. She was a teacher and reading consultant for many years, and is the author of numerous books for young readers.

Something Queer AT THE HAUNTED SCHOOL

by
Elizabeth Levy

illustrated by
Mordicai Gerstein

A Young Yearling Book

Published by
Dell Publishing
a division of
The Bantam Doubleday Dell Publishing Group, Inc.
666 Fifth Avenue
New York, New York 10103

From E. L.
To the Campus School and Dr. Sugarman

From M. G.
To the Evergreen Avenue School

Text copyright © 1982 by Elizabeth Levy
Illustrations copyright © 1982 by Mordicai Gerstein

For information address Delacorte Press, New York, New York.

The trademark Yearling® is registered in the U.S. Patent
and Trademark Office.

ISBN: 0-440-48461-8

Reprinted by arrangement with Delacorte Press
Printed in the United States of America
June 1983

19 18 17 16 15 14

CW

Gwen and Jill were planning their Halloween costumes. "What do you think Fletcher would want to be for Halloween?" asked Jill.

There were so many possibilities.

Fletcher Snail

Fletcher Roller Disco Star

Fletcher Fire
Hydrant

Fletcher Whale

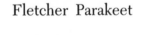

Fletcher Parakeet

Fletcher Lion

Fletcher Snake

Fletcher Shark

Fletcher Giraffe

Fletcher Ghost

Fletcher Vampire

"I've got it! A vampire!" exclaimed Jill. Fletcher wagged his tail. Fletcher hated to move, but he actually got up and licked Jill's face.

"He must really want to be a vampire!" said Gwen.

The next day, after school, Gwen and Jill got permission from their art teacher, Ms. Willoughby, to stay late and make Fletcher's costume. She let them bring Fletcher so they could be sure his costume fit. Then she left them alone to go to her studio.

FLETCHER'S VAMPIRE COSTUME!

THE BAT WINGS ARE CUT FROM CARDBOARD AND PAINTED BLACK. THEY'RE SEWN ON TO A BLACK CAPE WITH A BRIGHT RED LINING.

HE ALSO HAS A RED BOW TIE. HIS WHISKERS ARE CURLED AND HIS FANGS ARE DRAWN ON WITH A RED MAKEUP PENCIL, BUT HE LIKES TO LICK THEM OFF.

EEAAAAAARRRRGGHAIIIIIIIIIIIIII!

Suddenly Gwen and Jill heard a bloodcurdling scream. Fletcher jumped into the air and right into Gwen's and Jill's arms.

Ms. Willoughby ran into the art room screaming. "Why did you sneak up behind me, pretending to be a ghost?" she demanded. "Why did you make that weird howling noise?"

"We haven't left the room," protested Gwen.

Ms. Willoughby looked as if she didn't believe them.

The next day in class, when Mr. Murdoch, Gwen and Jill's history teacher, went to erase the blackboard, the whole class screamed. The words WEREWOLF POWER appeared as if written by a ghostly hand.

Mr. Murdoch dropped the eraser.

All that week a ghost seemed to be haunting the school. At first everyone thought a child was doing it, but no child could

1. hang all the flags upside down every morning.

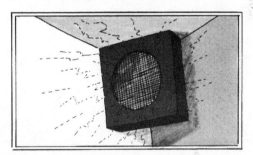

2. make weird howling noises come out of the public-address system.

3. cause strange glowing lights to dance across the stage during a class play about Greek gods.

Soon newspaper and TV reporters came to investigate the strange hauntings. Mr. Murdoch went out to talk to them.

"I have been doing some research," he said.

"Nearly one hundred years ago a young woman became possessed by demons on the very site on which this school was built. People believed she turned herself into a werewolf."

"A werewolf!" cried Jill. "Can you believe it!"

"No," said Gwen flatly. "Meet me in the school library."

Later in the day, Jill found Gwen up to her ears in books about hauntings, werewolves, and Halloween. "What are you doing?" asked Jill.

"Research," answered Gwen. "I don't believe in ghosts or werewolves. I think something queer is going on." Gwen tapped her braces. She always tapped her braces whenever something queer was going on.

"Everyone thinks something queer is going on," said Jill.

"But I don't think it's a supernatural kind of queer," said Gwen with a tap.

Suddenly from within the wall next to Gwen came an answering ghostly sound: *Tap . . . tap . . . TAP*.

Gwen's knees began to shake.

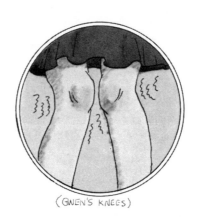

(GWEN'S KNEES)

Gwen and Jill ran to the room next door, but it was empty. It looked as if no *person* could have made those taps.

"*Now* do you believe in ghosts?" cried Jill.

"I don't know what to believe," said Gwen.

"I think we should tell Mr. Murdoch what happened," said Jill.

Mr. Murdoch had left school for the day. Gwen and Jill picked up Fletcher at Jill's house and walked him to Mr. Murdoch's house.

Mr. Murdoch had two names by his bell, MURDOCH/ ROSS.

"I thought Mr. Murdoch was a bachelor," said Gwen.

"Don't be so nosy," said Jill.

Mr. Murdoch was surprised to see them. He had a set of blueprints on his desk, which he put hastily into a drawer.

"Just looking at the plans for my dream house," he said. "What can I do for you?"

Gwen explained about the mysterious tapping in the library.

Mr. Murdoch was very excited by her news. "Historically ghosts often communicate by taps," he said. "I'm going to look into these tappings very closely."

As they left Mr. Murdoch's house Jill was so scared, she thought she saw ghostly werewolves behind every tree.

"There's got to be a rational explanation," muttered Gwen. "Someone wants us to think the school is haunted."

"Or it really *is* haunted," added Jill.

The next day Gwen and Jill went back to the library. Gwen was sure she had missed something. Suddenly she slammed one of the books down on the table and started tapping her braces.

This time there was no answering tap.

."Look at this!" exclaimed Gwen, showing Jill *The Haunted Laundromat* by Veronica Ross. "It was written before we were born, but it's about a Laundromat near us. It's the only other local haunting I've read about. I think we should investigate."

After school Gwen, Jill, and Fletcher took off for the Laundromat across town. The Laundromat *looked* haunted. It was shabby and full of cobwebs. A bell rang as they opened the door.

An old man came out of the back room. "Do you girls have laundry?" he asked hopefully.

Gwen shook her head no. "Is this the Laundromat that's supposed to be haunted?" she asked.

"OH, NO!" screamed the man so loudly that he scared Fletcher, who started to shake. "I thought after ten years everyone had forgotten."

"Forgotten what?" asked Gwen.

"About that horrible book," said the man.

His voice was so loud that his wife came running from the back. "Be careful, Sam," she warned. "Remember your heart."

"That book ruined our lives," said the man. "Our Laundromat was never haunted. Somebody just made it all up. We never met that woman—Veronica Ross, the author."

"Ross!" whispered Gwen. "I thought it sounded familiar." Gwen began to tap her braces.

"Why is she doing that?" asked the owner.

"She's thinking," explained Jill.

Finally Halloween arrived. The school was holding a big party, and everyone in town wanted to come to see what horrible spooky things the ghost would do.

Gwen and Jill went up to the art room to put the final touches on their costumes. They had made themselves vampire costumes too.

Ms. Willoughby admired their work. "I like the way you made a plan before you began, almost like a blueprint."

"A blueprint! I bet there's a clue in the blueprints," exclaimed Gwen. "Ms. Willoughby, can you get us blueprints of the school? It's important."

"It just so happens the blueprints are stored in the art department because we have the long flat files for them," said Ms. Willoughby. "I have a set in the bottom drawer."

Gwen and Jill studied the blueprints. "These stairs aren't here today," said Jill, pointing to some lines on the blueprints.

"Those are the old fire stairs," said Ms. Willoughby. "They were closed when we built the annex, but the stairs open onto the roof, right near the little room that I use for my studio."

CLOSE-UP OF THE FIRE STAIRS IN THE BLUEPRINTS

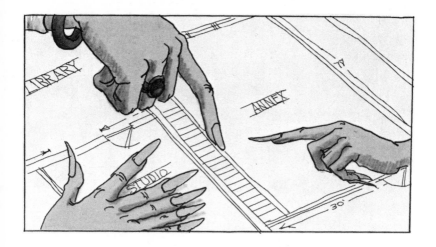

"Excellent!" said Gwen, with a tap to her fang. "Someone howled at you from the stairs."

"The stairs go right by the library," added Jill. "He or she could tap as well as howl."

"We can catch that someone tonight," said Gwen. She whispered her plan to Ms. Willoughby and Jill.

(THEY LISTEN CLOSELY. IT'S HARD TO UNDERSTAND GWEN WHEN SHE WEARS HER FANGS.)

Ms. Willoughby dressed up as a major league ball-player for the Halloween party. She carried a bat. In the middle of the party Gwen and Jill went up to her.

"It's time," whispered Gwen.

Ms. Willoughby nodded. She took Gwen, Jill, and Fletcher, all dressed as vampires, up to the school roof. However, Gwen was one vampire who carried a flashlight.

Suddenly they heard a
spooky howling sound.

"Is that Fletcher?" asked Jill
hopefully.

Gwen looked down at
Fletcher. He wasn't making
any noise.

"It's not Fletcher," said
Gwen. "Come on!"

Gwen opened the door to the secret stairwell. Something huge and hairy jumped out at them.

"YIKES!" shouted Jill. "A WEREWOLF!"

"A human werewolf!" shouted Gwen. "Don't let it get away." Ms. Willoughby waved her baseball bat at the creature. It growled and leaped back down the stairwell.

"After it!" shouted Gwen.
They chased the creature
back down the stairs
and into the party.

Many people had come dressed as werewolves, and for a moment Gwen and Jill lost their creature in the crowd.

"THERE IT IS!" yelled Jill, spotting the creature's big feet near the stage.

Gwen and Jill chased it all around the party and finally cornered it right in the middle of the stage.

"TAKE OFF YOUR WEREWOLF COSTUME, YOU FAKE!" Gwen demanded.

Jill reached over and tore the werewolf head off the cowering form. It was Mr. Murdoch.

Ms. Willoughby went to the microphone. "GWEN AND JILL HAVE EXPOSED THE WEREWOLF GHOST!" she said, as her voice boomed out over the public-address system. "THE SCHOOL IS NOT HAUNTED."

(GWEN TOOK HER FANGS OUT SO SHE COULD SPEAK MORE CLEARLY.)

Ms. Willoughby handed the microphone to Gwen, who blushed. Mr. Murdoch glared at her.

"My research has paid off," said Gwen. "Ten years ago, under the name of Veronica Ross, Mr. Murdoch wrote a book, *The Haunted Laundromat*. He made it all up. The Laundromat was never haunted. Jill and I saw the name *Ross* on Mr. Murdoch's doorbell. We figured out he was planning on writing a new book, *The Haunted School*."

"I needed the money to build my dream house," sniveled Mr. Murdoch. "I wanted to write another best seller."

"You scared innocent people," said Jill. "You used the old stairwell to create ghostly happenings."

"You even hid a piece of chalk in an eraser to write 'Werewolf Power,'" said Gwen.

ERASER

CHALK →

"I'll see that you get fired," said the principal.

"Someday I'd like to come back and haunt you," hissed Mr. Murdoch to Gwen.

"Luckily I don't believe in ghosts or werewolves," said Gwen.

WOOOOOWLLHOOWWLLLL

Suddenly everyone heard a faint, mysterious howling. The room grew quiet. Gwen and Jill looked down at Fletcher.

He was howling in his sleep.

Gwen and Jill patted him on the head. Fletcher rolled over and then seemed to smile. His nightmare was over.